D1597079

HOW TO CARE FOR YOUR NEW PET

CARING FOR
MY NEW
IGUANA

John Bankston

Mitchell Lane

PUBLISHERS

2001 SW 31st Avenue
Hallandale, FL 33009
www.mitchelllane.com

First Edition, 2021.

Author: John Bankston
Designer: Ed Morgan
Editor: Morgan Brody

Names/credits:
Title: Caring for My New Iguana / by John Bankston
Description: Hallandale, FL : Mitchell Lane Publishers

Series: How to Care for Your New Pet

Library bound ISBN: 978-1-58415-160-9

eBook ISBN: 978-1-58415-161-6

Photo credits: Freepik.com, Shutterstock

CONTENTS

Words in **bold**
throughout can be
found in the Glossary.

Wild Iguanas

Have you ever wanted a dragon? You won't find dragons at pet stores. You might find an iguana. With spiky backs and puffed-up throats, iguanas look like dragons. But they won't set your house on fire when they sneeze.

Most pets are tame. People began raising dogs and cats thousands of years ago. Iguanas are different. They have never been **domesticated**. Owning an iguana is like taking care of a wild animal. Because large reptiles can be **intimidating**, it may be important to have the support of an adult who can help with their care.

Iguanas can be difficult. They need very warm spaces. Adult iguanas need room to roam. Take your time before getting an iguana. Make sure you learn all about their **habits**.

DID YOU KNOW?

The Iguanodon (igwan–A–don) was a dinosaur that lived over 100 million years ago. It was 30 feet long. Its name means "iguana tooth."

Iguana Info

There are over 600 iguana **species** in the world. Green iguanas are the most **popular** pets. Adults grow to six feet long. They can weigh 20 pounds.

Wild green iguanas live in Mexico and parts of South America. They also thrive in Hawaii and Florida. Iguanas are not **native** to those states. Pet iguanas were released by careless owners.

Iguanas are reptiles. They are cold-blooded. They need sun to keep warm. Wild iguanas live in deserts and jungles. They hate the cold.

Green iguanas have spines from the neck to the tail. Their neck has a thick pocket of skin called a **dewlap**. The tail is twice as long as its body. It is a powerful weapon.

Green iguanas are bright green. They have dark stripes on their tails. Some are blue or greenish blue.

Marine iguanas are the only lizards to feed and live in the ocean. The rhino iguana looks like it has horns on the end of its nose. Blue iguanas live up to their name. They are bright blue! Many iguanas are called something else. The chuckwalla is a one-foot long iguana that lives in the southwest U.S. It inflates like a balloon.

DID YOU KNOW?

Did you know that an iguana was used in the movie Godzilla? This fictitious giant reptile who terrorized and destroyed entire cities was a marine iguana.

Living with Iguanas

Iguanas need space. If you plan to bring home a baby, get a **terrarium**. This glass box is like an aquarium. Instead of adding water, you'll add things like newspaper or brown wrapping paper. You can also use orchid barks or alfalfa pellets (rabbit pellets). One side should have food and water bowls. Bowls should be cleaned daily.

The terrarium should be kept in a warm part of the house. Place it on a sturdy table or desk. It should not be near windows or air conditioning.

How big should the terrarium be? Baby iguanas do well in a 30-gallon tank. When they are three-feet long, you will need to move them to a 55-gallon tank. Don't put baby iguanas in a tank that large. They might have trouble finding their food. At four feet, your iguana will need a room of his own.

DID YOU KNOW?

In the U.S., nearly two million homes have at least one pet reptile. Green iguanas are by far the most popular.

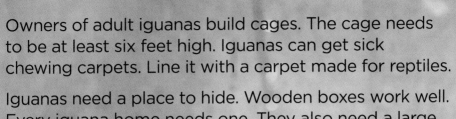

Owners of adult iguanas build cages. The cage needs to be at least six feet high. Iguanas can get sick chewing carpets. Line it with a carpet made for reptiles.

Iguanas need a place to hide. Wooden boxes work well. Every iguana home needs one. They also need a large bowl of water, so they don't get too dry.

The iguana home is his **habitat**. It should look like his home in the wild. He'll need a place to climb. This is how iguanas get away from danger. Iguana owners often find their pets **lurking** on a closet shelf or atop a refrigerator. Therefore, you'll want branches or ramps inside its cage. You can also add a few plants and rocks. This helps it look like the jungle.

Remember, your cold-blooded iguana needs a place to warm up. That is why UVA and UVB light is important. This special bulb acts like the sun. It should be placed over the tank, not in it. Part of the tank can then get up to 95 degrees Fahrenheit. This will be its place to **bask**.

The other part of the terrarium can be around 75 degrees Fahrenheit. No part of the iguana's living area should be colder than that. Don't put anything that heats up inside the terrarium. Your iguana could get burned. Switch off the lights at night. Get new bulbs every six months.

Once you have set up the iguana's home, it is time to find an iguana to fill it.

Finding Your Iguana

Choosing an iguana is not like picking a puppy. It's not going to come up to you and wag its tail. Choosing means asking questions. Pet stores sometimes sell iguanas. See if they can tell you where it comes from. Is it okay with people? Can you hold it? Notice how it acts when you do.

Breeders also raise and sell iguanas. They should know about their lizard's history. The cages should be clean. The iguana should not look skinny. The breeder can help you choose one that does well with people.

Iguanas grow. Full grown iguanas are often given up. Animal shelters may not have iguanas. Still there are many places to **adopt** one. Taking in an adult iguana isn't easy. It will need lots of space. It will also need time to get used to you. Adopting means giving a new home to a pet that doesn't have a place to live.

DID YOU KNOW?

Iguanas can grow a new tail. The new tail is not as colorful and doesn't have bones like their first tail.

Training Iguanas

Imagine you are your iguana. You've been moved from a pet store or a breeder to a new home. Everything is strange. You're scared. A large shadow falls across your body. You look up. What is this huge creature? Does it want to eat me?

Calm your iguana. Don't rush. Start by picking out its name. Use it often. Iguanas can learn their name. When you put down food or fresh water, talk to your iguana. Let it get used to you. They will soon look up when they see you.

Always wash your hands before spending time with your iguana. Wash them afterward, too. Iguanas can carry **salmonella**. It can also be found in their droppings. Salmonella can make you very sick. Kissing an iguana is always a bad idea.

Think about wild iguanas. **Predators** approach from above. That's why iguanas climb. Don't lower your hand over your iguana. Instead, move it slowly beside the iguana. Take your time. If it twitches its tail or expands its dewlaps, it's scared. Back off a bit but try again. Make sure your movements are slow. You don't want to quit. If you do, your iguana will learn that twitching its tail makes you leave. If you are patient, you will be able to pet it.

Watch your iguana. Is it twitching its tail quickly? Does it look like its squinting? This can mean it is ready to attack. Never pick it up or pet it when it is acting this way.

After a few weeks, try picking it up. Hold smaller ones by putting your hand under its belly. Larger ones will need to be held with another hand near the upper tail part. Make sure the room you are in has closed doors and no places for it escape.

If it gets away from you, don't panic and chase it. Let the iguana calm down and approach slowly speaking quietly. Don't race after it and don't grab it by the tail. If you do, your new pet might release its tail.

Iguanas have sharp teeth and claws. Their tails are covered with spikes. Going slowly will help keep you from getting hurt. If you take your time, you will soon have a pet that enjoys being close to you. Some owners say their pets have become "lap iguanas."

DID YOU KNOW?

Iguanas use their dewlap to catch warmer air. This helps it warm up in the morning.

Iguana Chow

Keep your pet iguana healthy and happy. Offer it the kind of food it would eat in the jungle or the desert. That means veggies. Lots and lots of veggies.

Green iguanas are **herbivores**. They only eat plants. Do not feed it crickets or other insects. Do not give it cat food. Iguana owners used to do that. It made their pets very sick.

Instead, buy fresh salad greens and other veggies. Have an adult help you wash and chop them. Iguanas don't chew. They swallow each bite. Make sure the veggies are small if you have a baby iguana.

Some iguana owners prepare several meals. Wrap a damp paper towel around some lettuce. Put it in a plastic bag and store it in your refrigerator.

Other iguana treats include dandelion greens, kale, and fresh parsley. Do not give them spinach. **Calcium** in milk gives you strong bones. Iguanas need calcium, too. Don't give them milk. Instead, sprinkle calcium powder on the iguana's food. Do this every other meal.

Fruit is okay as a special snack once a week. Iguanas like bananas, strawberries and apples.

Some meals can come from pet food made for iguanas. Check that it doesn't have insects or other meat. Let your iguana eat all the lettuce they like. It won't make them fat. Iguanas like a big breakfast. Give them most of their food in the morning after they wake up.

Make sure they have lots of fresh water, too. Baby iguanas may have a hard time finding the water bowl. Get a sprayer to mist them.

Never give your iguana potato chips or any kind of chocolate or other sugary treats. Never give them coffee, tea or soda either.

Some other kinds of iguanas do eat insects or meat. If your pet is not a green iguana, you will need to learn its exact diet.

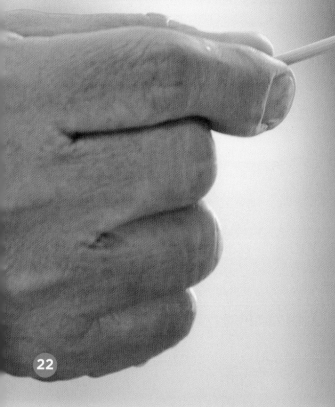

Your Healthy Iguana

Pet iguanas can live for over twenty years. Many do not live this long. This is because of the food their owners fed them. Besides giving them the best food, make sure your iguana gets checkups and yearly exams.

The week you bring home your iguana, take it to the **veterinarian**. This is a doctor just for animals. Many vets do not treat iguanas. You will need one that takes care of reptiles.

Iguanas can get sick from eating meat. That is why the vet will check its kidneys. Iguanas often have bone problems because they do not get enough calcium.

Take good care of your iguana. Give it the right food and spend lots of time with it and you will enjoy many happy years with a very unusual pet.

SHOPPING LIST

This is a list of some things your iguana will need:

- ☐ Terrarium 30 to 100 gallons (depending on the iguana's size)

- ☐ Adult iguanas need a cage that is at least eight feet long, three feet wide and six feet tall.

- ☐ Thermometers to check the terrarium's temperature

- ☐ UVA and UVB lightbulbs

- ☐ Water and food bowls

- ☐ Ramps and branches

- ☐ A wooden box for hiding

- ☐ Newspapers, paper towels or "reptile" carpet for the bottom of the cage

- ☐ Spray bottle or water tub

FIND OUT MORE

Online
There are many sites that will help you raise happy, healthy iguanas:

The Resource for Iguana Care and Adoption has information on their care and training:
http://iguanaresource.org/socialization.html

Petfinder connects people with adoptable animals. They have iguanas in their "scales, skins and others" section:
https://www.petfinder.com/search/scales-fins-others-for-adoption/?sort%5B0%5D=recently_added

Books

Collard, Sneed B., *One Iguana, Two Iguanas.* Thomaston, Maine: Tilbury House Publishers. 2018.

Connors, Kathleen. *Iguanas.* New York: Gareth Stevens Pub., 2013.

Lunis, Natalie. Green. *Iguanas*. New York, N.Y. : Bearport Pub., 2010.

GLOSSARY

adoption
Taking care of someone without a family

bask
Lie out in the sun

breeders
People who spend a lot of time caring for animals

calcium
Mineral that helps build strong bones

dewlap
Fold of loose skin that hangs from an animal's throat

domesticated
Tame, used to people

habits
Regular behavior

habitat
Natural home of an animal

herbivores
Animal that only eats plants

intimidating
To make someone afraid

lurking
To be in a hidden place

native
Coming from a certain place

popular
Well-liked

predator
Animal that preys on other animals

salmonella
Bacteria that can make people very sick, usually found in food

species
A group of similar animals

terrarium
A glass tank for smaller reptiles

veterinarian
Doctor who specializes in animal care

BIBLIOGRAPHY

"About the Green Iguana." *National Geographic*. https://www.nationalgeographic.com/animals/reptiles/g/green-iguana/

"Best Iguana Cage Reviews 2019: The Best Choice for Your Pet." *My Life Pets*. May 8, 2019. https://mylifepets.com/best-iguana-cage/

Crutchfield, Tom. "Green Iguana Care Sheet." *Reptile Magazine*. http://www.reptilesmagazine.com/Care-Sheets/Lizards/Green-Iguana/

Darling, Leslie. "Five Most Common House Pets." *The Nest*. https://pets.thenest.com/5-common-house-pets-4759.html

"Five Core Elements of Iguana Husbandry." Resource for Iguana Care and Adoption. http://iguanaresource.org/feltsofiguanacare.html

"Galapagos Pink Land Iguana." Galapagos Conservation Trust. https://galapagosconservation.org.uk/wildlife/galapagos-pink-land-iguana/

"Green Iguana: Iguana iguana." *PetMD*. https://www.petmd.com/reptile/species/green-iguana

"Iguana Care Guide." *VetBabble*. March 24, 2019. https://www.vetbabble.com/reptiles/iguana-care/

Kruzer, Adrienne, RVT, LVT. "Green Iguanas: The Basics of Pet Green Iguanas." *The Spruce Pets*. February 17, 2017. https://www.thesprucepets.com/green-iguanas-1239136

McLeod, DVM. Lianne. "A Guide to Caring for Iguanas as Pets." *The Spruce Pets*. January 12, 2019. https://www.thesprucepets.com/iguanas-as-pets-1236880

"How to Train Your Pet Iguana." *The Spruce Pets*. February 10, 2019. https://www.thesprucepets.com/handling-pet-iguanas-1236878

"Why Do Pet Reptiles Need Heat and Light?" *The Spruce Pets*. May 5, 2019. https://www.thesprucepets.com/reptiles-light-and-heat-1237231

Miller, Kyle. "A Keeper's Favorite Grand Cayman Blue Iguana Facts." Smithsonian National Zoo. March 3, 2017. https://nationalzoo.si.edu/animals/news/keepers-favorite-grand-cayman-blue-iguana-facts

Osterloff, Emily. "Iguanodo : the Teeth that Led to a Dinosaur Discovery." Natural History Museum. November 8, 2018. https://www.nhm.ac.uk/discover/the-discovery-of-iguanodon.html

"Reptile Ownership Drops, Research Firm Says." *Reptile Magazine*. http://www.reptilesmagazine.com/Reptile-Ownership-Drops-Research-Firm-Says/

"Reptiles: Rhino Iguana." Australia Zoo. https://www.australiazoo.com.au/our-animals/reptiles/lizards/rhino-iguana

INDEX

ABOUT THE AUTHOR

John Bankston

The author of over 100 books for young readers, John Bankston lives in Miami Beach, Florida with his rescue dog Astronaut. Walking around South Florida he often sees green iguanas. He really enjoyed writing a book that gave him a chance to learn all about these reptiles.